One yellow day
one hot day
one blue day
one cold day
one scary day
one curious day
the circus
the lightning-bolted
striped-tented demented
circus
swept
leapt
somersaulted
cartwheeled
and flipped
into my town
my small town
big town
dusty street
green field
singing dancing cavorting eyes my ears my head my heart
into my
roaring
tiptoeing and altogether

The crowd was fidgeting.

Chattering.

The lights went down.

The hush descended. Then . . .

CRASH

HORNS

BLARE BOO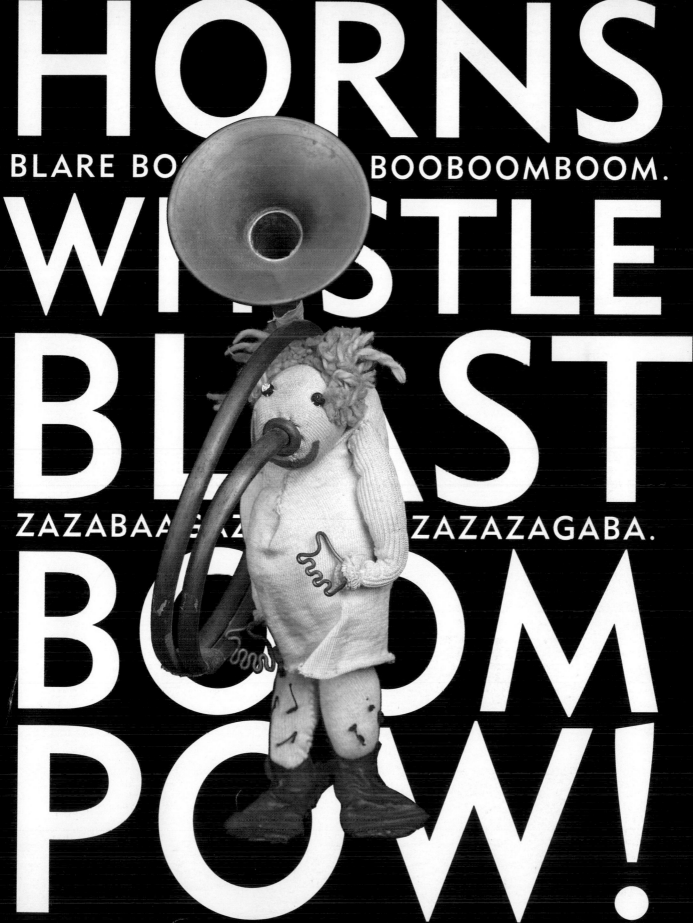BOOBOOMBOOM.

WHISTLE

BLAST

ZAZABAAZAZAZAGABA.

BOOM

POW!

"LADIES AND GENTLEMEN"...

Thank you, Emily Oberman, David Ross, Jennifer Russell, and Charlotte Sheedy for help and encouragement, and the Whitney Museum art handlers for careful patience with the photography process.

Photographs: Front endleaf © Ugo Mulas; Back endleaf © Ugo Mulas; Back cover © Marvin Schwartz; Calder biography © The Estate of Andre Kertesz; Text © 1991 Maira Kalman; Photographs © 1991 Donatella Brun; © 1991 Whitney Museum of American Art, 945 Madison Avenue, New York, New York 10021.
Published by Delacorte Press, Bantam Doubleday Dell Publishing Group, Inc., 1540 Broadway, New York, New York 10036.
Printed in New York by D.L. Terwilliger Sterling-Roman.
Manufactured in the United States of America.

Library of Congress Cataloging in Publication Data

Kalman, Maira.
  Roarr: Calder's Circus / by Maira Kalman with photography by Donatella Brun.
  p. 32 21.3 x 27.9 cm
  Summary:
  The Calder Circus comes roaring into town to razzle dazzle those of all ages.
  ISBN 0-385-30916-3
  [1. Circus—Fiction.] I. Brun, Donatella. ill. II. Whitney Museum of American Art.
III. Title.
PZ7.K1256Ro 1991
[E]—dc20   91-33745   CIP   AC

May 1993

10 9 8 7 6 5 4 3 2 1

FSL

ROARR: CALDER'S CIRCUS

A Story by Maira Kalman

Photographs by Donatella Brun

Designed by M&Co

Delacorte Press/
Whitney Museum of American Art

It's Monsieur Loyal, the long-winded ringmaster,

"Preposterous people, ridiculous rascals, and colicky children of all ages.

We proudly present to you the stupendous, stupefying

and stupid... I mean salubrious... I mean superlative

Calder Circus

that will razzle dazzle and frazzle you to your very toes."

The crowd cheered. The dogs barked.

One boy hit another boy over the head with a shoe.

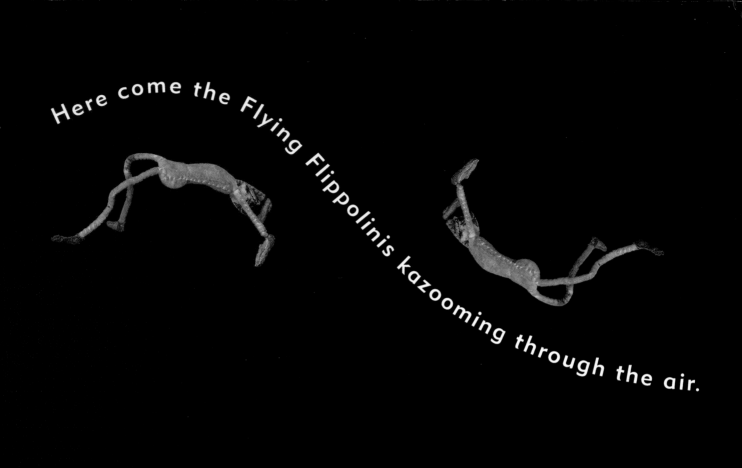

Here come the Flying Flippolinis kazooming through the air.

hey! Daddy longlegs there's a bicycle going through your

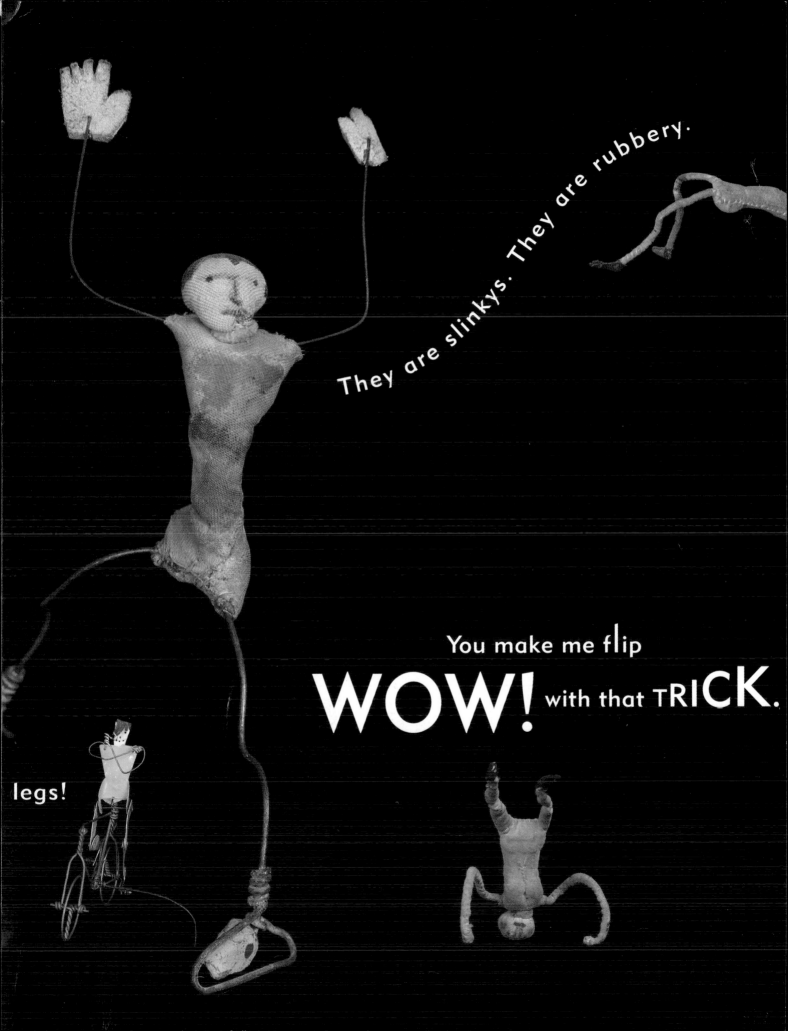

CRRRA

The brave
lion tamer will
stick his head into the
mouth of the mean
and ferocious…

Miss Tamara

No, you nincompoop.

CK K! of the whip!

Not the dog! Into the **lion's** mouth.
Have you ever stuck
your head into
the mouth of a lion?
It's dark. It's wet.
It's sharp.
It's not where you want to be.

"Ramona

Suddenly this devilish clown, this black-hatted Cativo

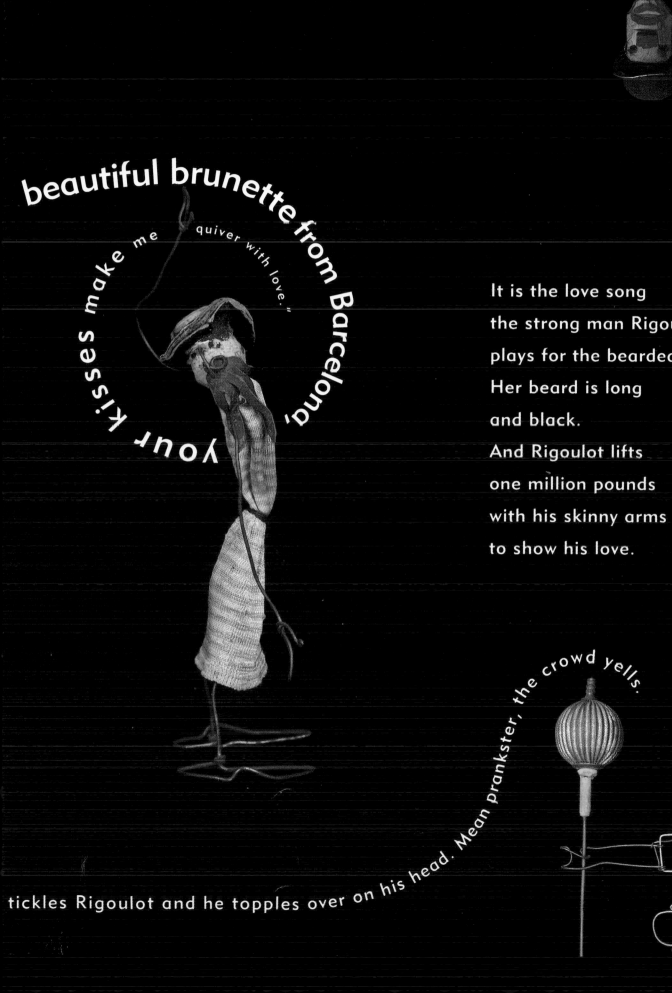

"beautiful brunette from Barcelona, your kisses make me quiver with love."

It is the love song
the strong man Rigoulot
plays for the bearded lady.
Her beard is long
and black.
And Rigoulot lifts
one million pounds
with his skinny arms
to show his love.

Mean prankster, the crowd yells.

tickles Rigoulot and he topples over on his head.

Now hoofbeats, clomping, clattering, dust kicked up. Yahoo. Lasso.

Texi's horse has **red** spots.

O.K. pardner.

Can a **horse** have **chicken** pox?

SILENCE!

(Please) The Maharajah
will throw his sword
just above the tranquil head
of the beautiful woman.

He needs

absolute concentration or else the lady will be a dead duck. He aims. He is about to throw.

Suddenly

a head-splitting

s n E E Z E

is heard.

Who?

Who is the culprit?

It is Cativo the clown.

This is not funny.

The curvaceous Madame Olga

is trilling her aria when **Cativo** starts howling like

Decline, reduce in

Desist!

Vanish!

Exit!

No? What a pity.

a hound. Enough, OLGA SHRILLS. You have made us mutts too nuts.

size. Become a dot. And now you nit become a NOT.

And Presto. Vanisho.
Good-bye Cativo.
On with the show.

Ladies and gentlemen, birdbrains and   flatfoots, juvenile   delinquents and tattle   tales of all ages. Presenting the world's tallest man. He towers over the trapeze and when he spits it rains on the peppy pup and the rhododendrons and chrysanthemum mum-mums.

Fanny is a belly dancer.

She has a wild belly and a wild button.

She has this thing this **ZING.**

The sword swallower cannot take his eyes off Fanny.

He makes a mistake with his sword
and now when he drinks water
he looks like a

fountain!

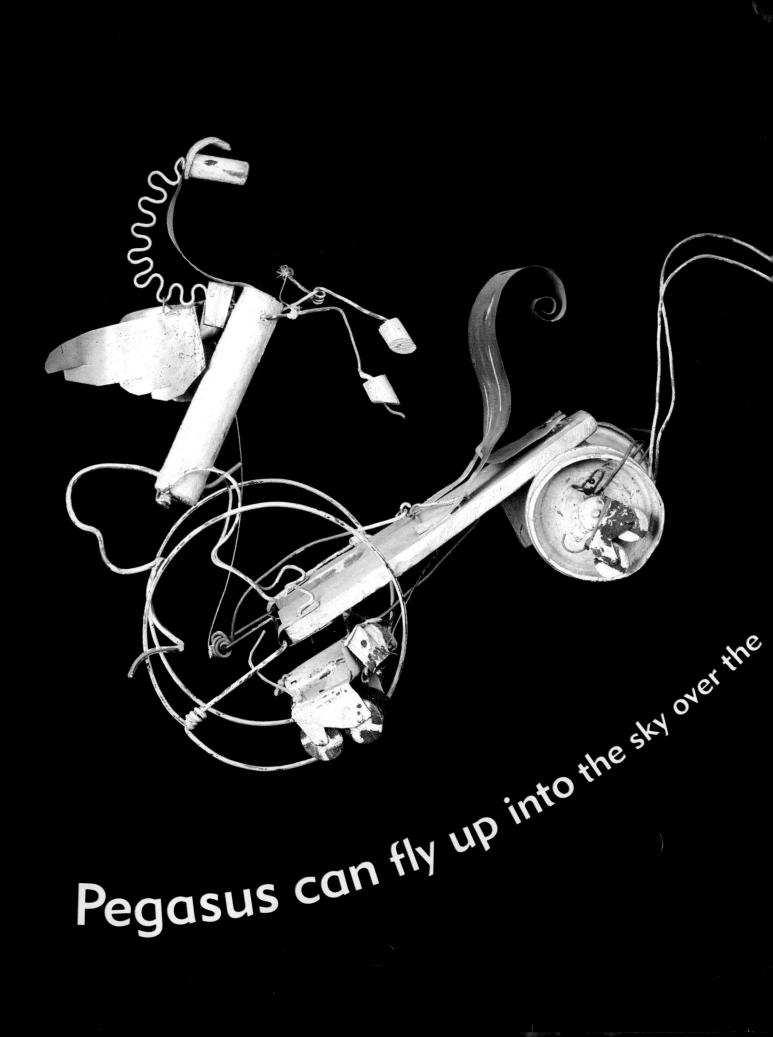

Pegasus can fly up into the sky over the

stars and the paper man can jump off the world. His dress is a parachute and he lands softly down.

Tiptoe, tip tip toeing, taking teeny tiny steps traversing the taut wire, the invisible thread that on

painted toes the tightrope walkers tread. Balance . . . . balance... balance, in the darkness, in the air.

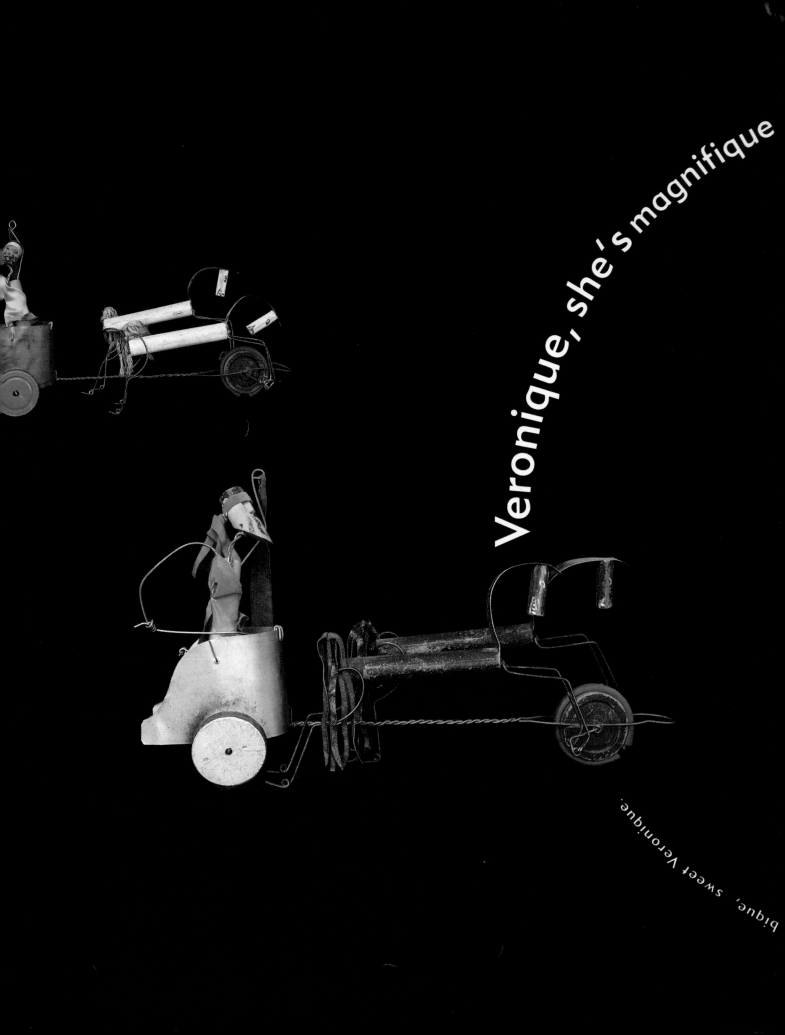

Veronique, she's magnifique

bique, sweet Veronique.

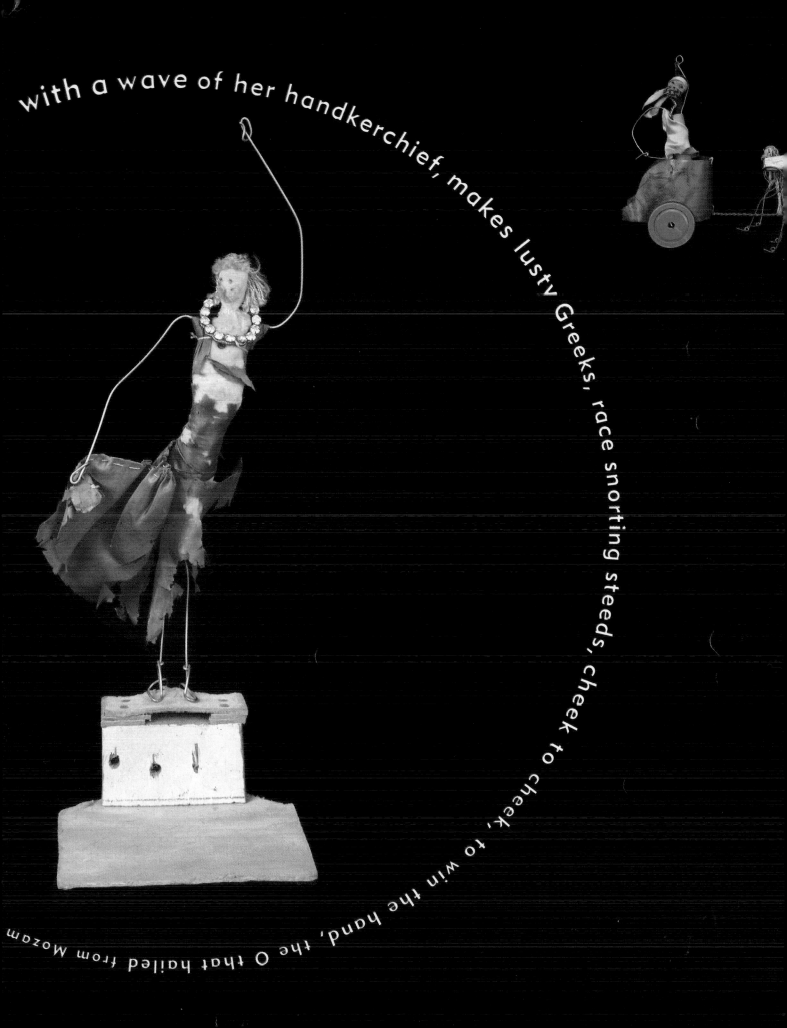

with a wave of her handkerchief, makes lusty Greeks, race snorting steeds, cheek to cheek to win the hand, the O that hailed from Mozam

the Calder Circus has come to an end.
We have shown you the moon and the stars.
We have shown you the happy and the sad.
Now we are on our way. The finale is here.
We are traveling to the distant shores
of Constantinople and invite you,
beseech you, implore you, each
babbling baby, each gnarled
geezer (and all goofballs in
between) to join us in our
fantastic gallivanting
to unknown
adventures
!

And with a flourish a wiggle and a wave

they were gone.
It was over.
We sat in stunned silence.
Feverish brains. Limpid limbs.
We sighed, stood, stretched.
Put on our hats.
Put on our coats.
Shuffled out into
the Prussian blue night
      the lime green day
            the hysterical city
                  the splashing stream
                        the windy rain
                              the gentle breeze thinking,

                        See you later circus.

See you in my dreams.

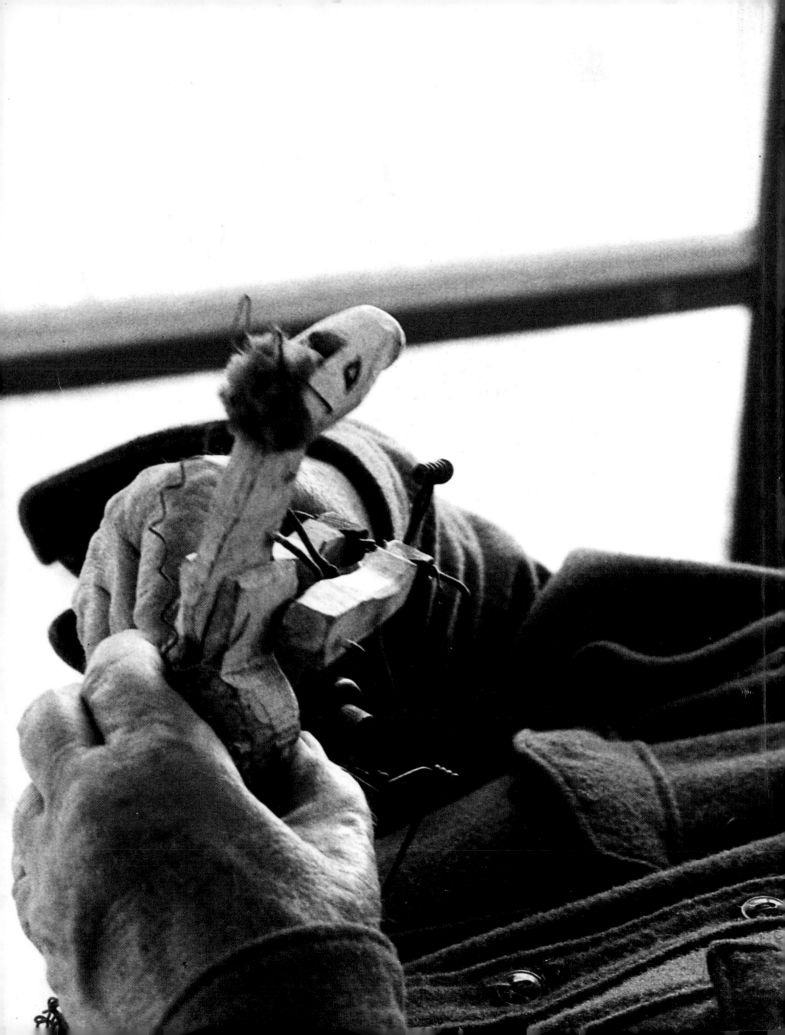